TRUMP FOR BLACKS

HIGHLIGHTS ON TRUMPS ACHIEVEMENTS IN THE BLACK COMMUNITY

ANGELA Y. NIXON

JG | Jenis Group, LLC

TRUMP FOR BLACKS
Copyright © 2017 by Angela Y. Nixon
Originall self-published in 2017

This book is a work of fiction. Names, characters, businesses, organizations, places, events and incidents either are the product of the author's imagination or are used fictitiously. Any resemblance to actual persons, living or dead, events, or locales is entirely coincidental.

Jenis Group, LLC Edoitions trade paperback edition November 2017

For information contact :
Jenis Group, LLC
http://www.jenisgroup.com

First Edition: November 2017

Manufactured in the Unted States of America

10 9 8 7 6 5 4 3 2 1

ISBN: 9781942674306

You're either part of the solution or part of the problem.
- (Leroy) Eldridge Cleaver (1935-1998)

TRUMP FOR BLACKS

HIGHLIGHTS ON TRUMPS ACHIEVEMENTS IN THE BLACK COMMUNITY

3

7

12

13

BLACKS FOR TRUMP

ANGELA Y. NIXON

23

ANGELA Y. NIXON

25

26

27

ANGELA Y. NIXON

BLACKS FOR TRUMP

ANGELA Y. NIXON

35

43

44

ANGELA Y. NIXON

47

ANGELA Y. NIXON

49

50

51

52

53

ANGELA Y. NIXON

56

59

61

62

67

69

75

78

81

91

93

95

105

ANGELA Y. NIXON

119

121

131

137

141

142

143

ANGELA Y. NIXON

151

157

159

169

181

9 781942 674306